LET'S TRY SOCCER!

By Susa Hämmerle

Illustrated by Kyrima Trapp

Translated by Marisa Miller

NorthSouth
BOOKS

New York / London

Luke was no longer allowed to play soccer in the house. Luke's right foot was to blame. It just wouldn't stop kicking. The other problem was Mom's expensive vase, which unfortunately met up with a flying soccer ball and now lay shattered in the trash can. Luke looked around, feeling bored. He saw two of Lisa's stuffed animals. The rabbit was round and soft. It flew through the air, almost like a soccer ball! Luke dribbled the rabbit. Then he set it up for a kick and "Goal!" shouted Luke. "Gooooaaal!"

His little sister, Lisa, came running in from the playroom. His mom came running from the kitchen.

"Mopsy isn't a soccer ball!" Lisa howled. She grabbed her stuffed animals and ran into the kitchen.

Mom shook her head. "We've got to get you playing soccer on a team," she said.

Luke was so excited he jumped into the air.

That evening when Dad came home, they talked it over. And it was decided. In two days, Luke would go to his first soccer practice!

Dad drove Luke to the soccer field. They walked over to the clubhouse. You could hear wild screaming and shouting from the locker room. Luke clutched his new cleats tightly to his chest. It sounded as though there were a hundred kids in there . . . but they all fell silent the minute he entered.

"Are you the new kid?" called a black-haired boy. Luke was much too nervous to say anything. Luckily, the coach came over. "Nice to see you, Luke," he said. Then he introduced him to the other kids. Most of them looked friendly. But the black-haired boy made Luke a little nervous!

cap

elbow pads

gloves

shin guards

cleats

The coach clapped his hands. "Let's warm up!" he cried.

The kids followed him onto the field. They jogged in a line around the center circle. When the coach blew the whistle, they froze.

Shyly, Luke joined in. He was having fun. But suddenly he realized something. "Where's my dad?" he shouted.

The girl in front of him turned around and smiled. She pointed to the substitutes' bench. There was Dad, sitting and watching.

Luke felt better. He followed along with the warm-up exercises. He swung his arms. He hopped up and down. He stretched and bent his legs. From time to time, he'd glance at the black-haired boy.

But the black-haired boy ignored Luke completely.

"Okay," said the coach. "Now your muscles and tendons are warm enough to practice with the ball. Everyone grab one!"

The children sprinted off.

Once everyone had a ball, the black-haired boy showed how to keep the ball in the air with your foot and switch it between two feet. Then he demonstrated how to keep the ball in the air with your head and how to control it behind your back.

Luke was impressed. "He's our best player," said the friendly girl. "Unfortunately, he's not always the nicest."

Luke didn't answer. He concentrated on the ball. And then he noticed that some of the kids were placing brightly colored cones on the soccer field.

"What are the cones for?" asked Luke.

"To dribble the ball around," said one of the boys. "You'll see—it's fun!"

The boy was right. When it was Luke's turn, he didn't want to stop.

foot reception

head reception

chest reception

Eventually the coach blew his whistle again. Now they practiced stopping the ball, passing it to a teammate, and finally kicking it into the goal.

Luke already felt like a real soccer player. His heart was beating fast. At last he'd be able to show off the power of his right foot!

One boy set the ball on the penalty spot. The
girl went into the goal. Luke set the ball in
place. He took a running start. And then—
"Bah! That little baby doesn't even know what
a goal is"—he heard the black-haired boy say,
and the ball flew just to the left of the goal.

No one laughed at Luke. No one called him a failure. In fact, the coach praised Luke for his strong kick.

Dad waved encouragingly.

But poor Luke felt awful.

"Chin up," said the coach. "Get ready for our practice match."

Luke certainly didn't want to miss that. His big dream was to play on a team with real fullbacks and forwards and everything!

The coach marked off half of the area as the playing field.

Two goals were quickly set up and positions were chosen. The black-haired boy was on defense. Luke was going to play center forward or striker on the opposing team. He was so excited, he forgot all about his missed goal. The whistled blasted, and they were off!

bicycle kick
and
GOOOAL!

The wind buzzed in his ears. He ran and stopped, zigzagged, ran, and suddenly he had the ball.

But the black-haired boy was there, too. He followed Luke like a shadow. Luke dribbled. Out of the corner of his eye, he saw Dad, who was jumping up and down, cheering Luke on.

header

push-pass

outside-of-foot kick

power-shot

Kicking foot forward! Luke told himself. And then: "Goal!" cried his team. "Goooal!"

Never in his life had Luke felt so proud. Everyone congratulated him—even the black-haired boy. His name was Nick .

"We could use you," said Nick. "I mean, once you know all the rules."

"That's why Luke is here." The coach laughed. "Why don't you come on Sunday, Luke? You can watch us play in a real game. You will learn a lot just by watching."

"We'll be there," said Dad. It was time to say good-bye. Luke's first soccer practice was over.

At last it was Sunday.

Mom and Lisa came with them to the soccer field.

It looked very different. There was a big crowd of people sitting on the bleachers. Some waved flags or waved to the mascots. Vendors sold refreshments. The referee stood next to the playing field, talking to the coaches. Then the teams ran out. Luke's team wore red uniforms.

"We have to cheer them on," said Luke. "That'll help them score more goals—oh!"

Someone had tapped him on the shoulder. It was Nick. "Do you have room for one more here?" he asked.

"Yes, of course," said Dad. "We always have room for a soccer expert."

"What's an expert?" whispered Luke.

"Somebody who knows all the ins and outs of the game," Dad whispered back.

"And someone who likes to explain things." Nick grinned. He sat down next to Luke.

"Hey, my kangaroo isn't a seat cushion!" cried Lisa.

But Nick didn't hear her. He only had eyes and ears for the game, which had just started.

So did Luke. And Dad, too . . .

red card

hand ball

direct kick

indirect kick

advantage clause

corner kick

offside

substitution

throw-in

There's a lot going on at the soccer field, whether in practice or in a game. And there are many special words that are used. Here are some of them:

soccer ball

Circumference must be between 27 in (68 cm) and 28 in (70 cm). Weight must be between 14 oz (410 g) and 16 oz (450 g).

dribbling

fan's flag

cones

lineman's flag

header

substitutes' bench

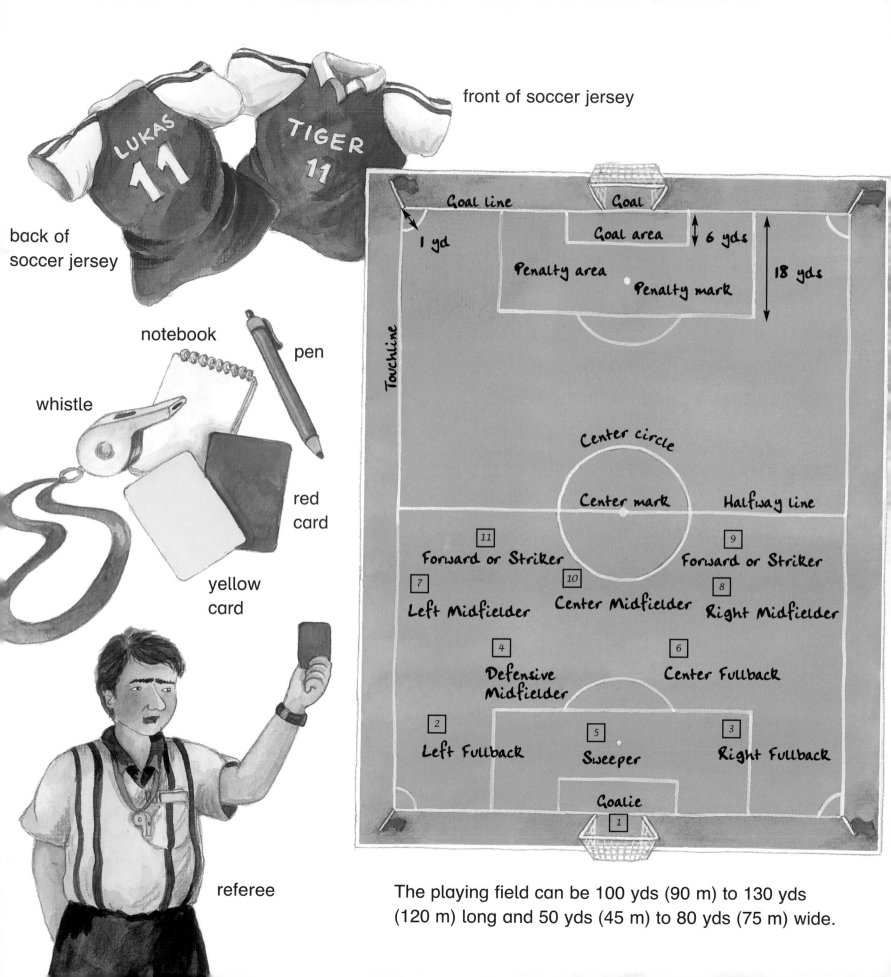

front of soccer jersey

back of
soccer jersey

LUKAS
11

TIGER
11

notebook

pen

whistle

red
card

yellow
card

referee

Goal line

Goal

1 yd

Goal area

6 yds

Penalty area

Penalty mark

18 yds

Touchline

Center circle

Center mark

Halfway line

11

Forward or Striker

9

Forward or Striker

7

Left Midfielder

10

Center Midfielder

8

Right Midfielder

4

Defensive
Midfielder

6

Center Fullback

2

Left Fullback

5

Sweeper

3

Right Fullback

Goalie

1

The playing field can be 100 yds (90 m) to 130 yds
(120 m) long and 50 yds (45 m) to 80 yds (75 m) wide.

Finish

Start